The friends of Apple Street

Anna Pignataro

Lothian BOOKS

Near Rippling Lake is
Apple Street.

That's where the six friends
Pug, Queenie, Lucy, Mango,
Bella and Eliza live.

Today the sun is shining
in Apple Street.

This is
Queenie's house.

Here is Queenie singing on the balcony.

This is Eliza's house.

Here is Eliza planting
poppies in the garden.

Poppy love

Here is Lucy **dancing** in the courtyard.

This is Bella's house.

Here is Bella riding her pony.

This is Mango's house.

Here is Mango
Playing the guitar.

This is
Pug's house.

Here is Pug building a boat.

Pitter, patter, plop, splat!
It's raining in Apple Street.

The friends play together in the Puddles and the raindrops.

SPLOSH!

Then Mango, Queenie, Eliza, Bella and Pug...

...all go to Lucy's house for tea and cupcakes.

For my little girl, who is all of the Apples;
for Mark, Mango and Pug;
for my gorgeous friends Veronica,
Betty, Angela and Shaney — thank you;
and for my goddaughter Floriana. A.P.

Thomas C. Lothian Pty Ltd
An imprint of Time Warner Book Group Australia
132 Albert Road, South Melbourne, Victoria 3205
www.lothian.com.au

Copyright © Anna Pignataro 2006

First published 2006

National Library of Australia Cataloguing-in-Publication data
Pignataro, Anna
  The Friends of Apple Street
  For children.

  ISBN 0 7344 0959 1.

  I. Title.

A823.4

Designed by Georgie Wilson
Illustration media: collage, watercolour, ink, acrylic and tempera
Colour reproduction by Hell Colour Australia
Printed in China by WKT